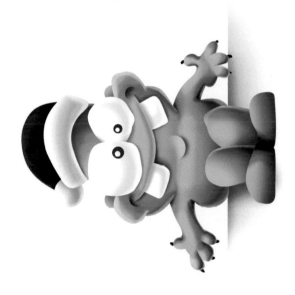

For Speedy, anything is possible – TM
For Levi (you should always blame your dad) – MS

ABC
Books

The ABC 'Wave' device and the ABC For Kids device are
trademarks of the Australian Broadcasting Corporation and are
used under licence by HarperCollins Publishers Australia.

First published in Australia in 2015
by HarperCollins Publishers Australia Pty Limited
ABN 36 009 913 517
harpercollins.com.au

HarperCollinsPublishers
Level 13, 201 Elizabeth Street, Sydney NSW 2000, Australia
Unit D1, 63 Apollo Drive, Rosedale, Auckland 0632, New Zealand
A 53, Sector 57, Noida, UP, India
1 London Bridge Street, London SE1 9GF, United Kingdom
2 Bloor Street East, 20th floor, Toronto, Ontario M4W 1A8, Canada
195 Broadway, New York NY 10007, USA

National Library of Australia Cataloguing-in-Publication entry:

Miller, Tim, author.
There is a monster under my Christmas tree who farts / Tim Miller ; Matt Stanton, illustrator.
ISBN: 978 0 7333 3295 1 (hardback)
For ages 4+.
Flatulence–Juvenile fiction.
Monsters–Juvenile fiction.
Stanton, Matt, illustrator.
Australian Broadcasting Corporation.

A823.4

Designed and typeset by Matt Stanton
The illustrations in this book were hand drawn and digitally coloured.
Colour reproduction by Graphic Print Group, Adelaide
Printed in China by RR Donnelley on 128gsm Matt Art

5 4 3 2 1   15 16 17

THERE IS A MONSTER UNDER MY CHRISTMAS TREE WHO FARTS

TIM MILLER + MATT STANTON

ABC
Books

There is a **monster** under my Christmas tree who farts.

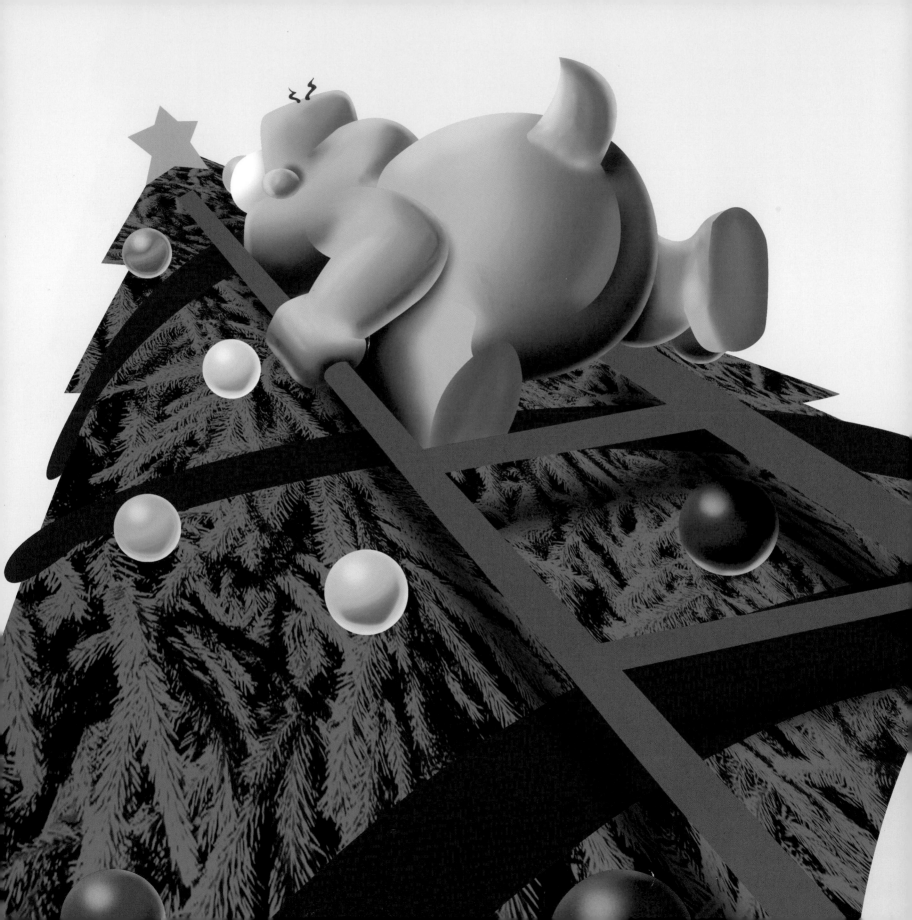

You don't want **his** help putting up the star.

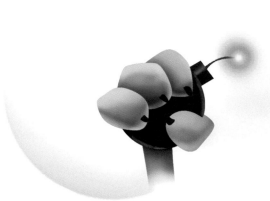

His **bauble bombs** smell so bad
I can't wrap presents in my room.

And his **bottom burps** will destroy the reindeers' carrots.

There is a **monster** in Santa's workshop who **farts**.

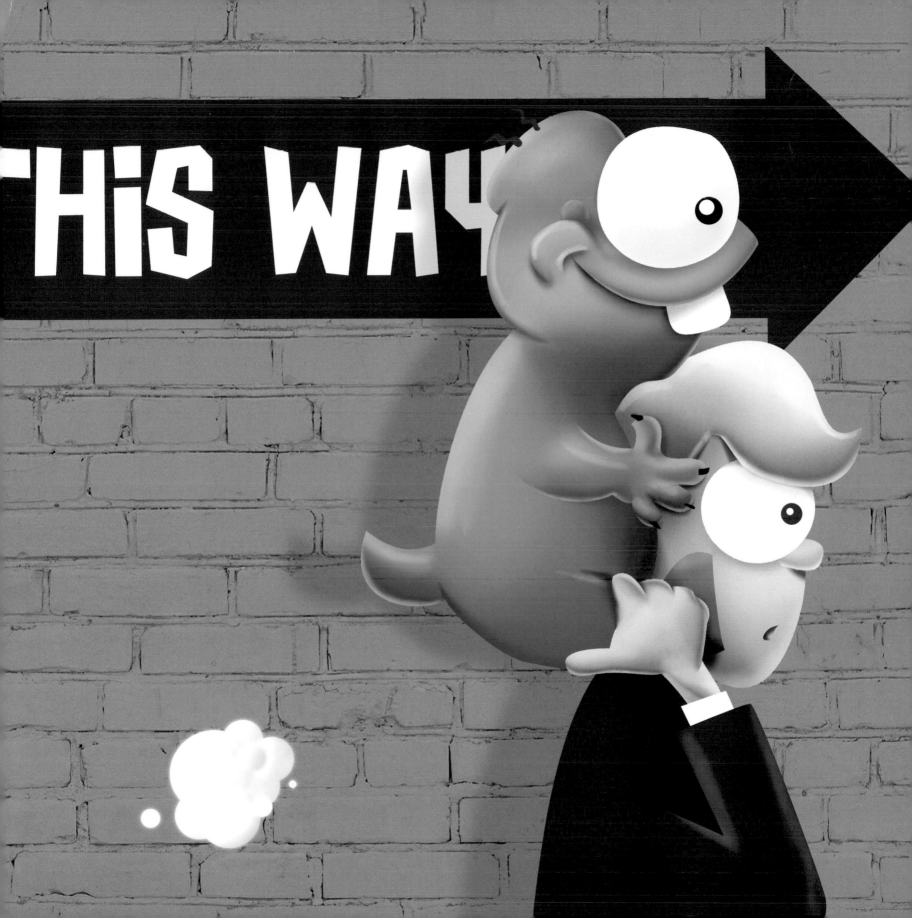

His **gas cloud** ruined
my special photo.

And he's **destroyed** everyone's Christmas cheer.

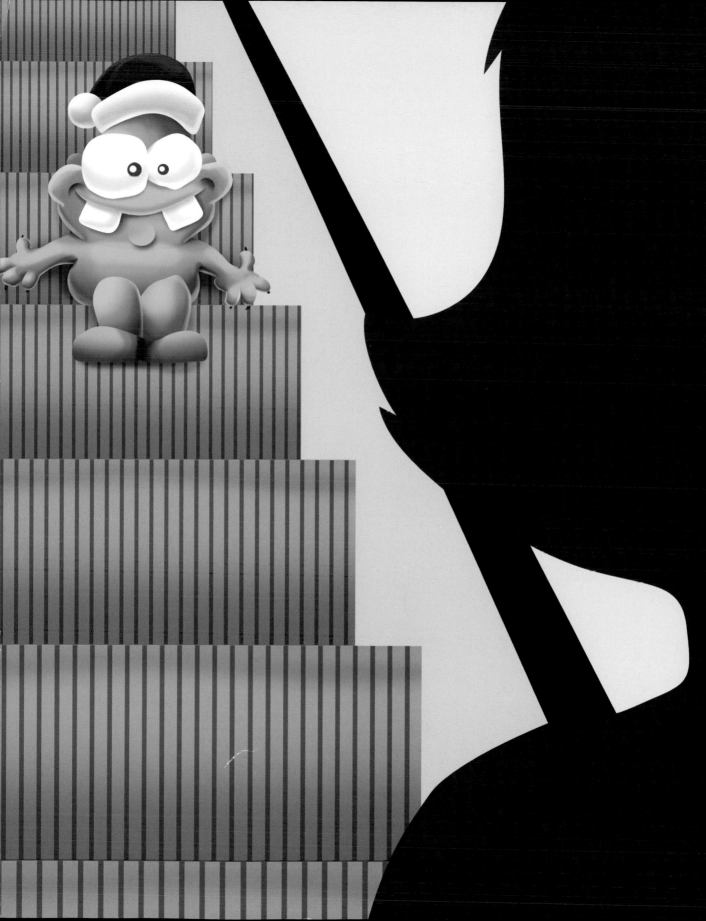

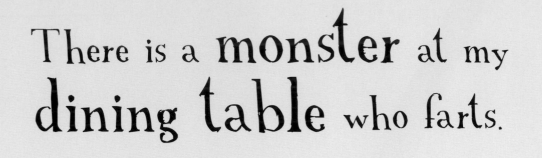

There is a **monster** at my
dining table who farts.

There is a **monster** on the **roof** who farts.

Dad can't hang the flashing lights!

There is a monster on my **front porch** who farts.

He's **scaring** off the Christmas carollers!

'Santa won't come!'